Chester
the Great

Weekly Reader Books presents

Chester the Great

(Original title: Chester)

Mary Francis Shura
Illustrated by Susan Swan

DODD, MEAD & COMPANY
NEW YORK

Library of Congress Cataloging in Publication Data

Shura, Mary Francis.
    Chester.

    SUMMARY: Nobody believed it was possible for just
one new kid to change a whole neighborhood in one week—
until Chester came.
    I. Swan, Susan Elizabeth. II. Title.
PZ7.S55983Ch   [Fic]   79-6633
ISBN 0-396-07800-1
ISBN 0-396-08631-4 (pbk.)

Cover illustration by Mike Eagle.

To the
Grands of Craigcroft
with
Love

Contents

Saturday

Chester moved into the Owens house on Saturday.

You wouldn't think it could make so much difference for just one new kid to move into the neighborhood, especially if he wasn't even down on our end of the street but up the hill behind the trees that hide the Owens house.

You would be wrong.

In one week, in one single week, Chester changed our neighborhood so much that it hasn't been the same since. And I don't think it ever *will* be the same again.

It wasn't just any old neighborhood that he changed, either. Every kid in the Millard C. Fillmore School District had heard about our neighborhood. We were known for having our own living, breathing *Guinness Book of World Records* in that block where we five all live.

Then Chester came on that Saturday.

I know for sure it was Saturday because I was cleaning my room. I never clean my room except on Saturday, and then only when Mom gets very high voiced and threatening.

I had already cleaned my room once when Mom came up for an inspection. I am not that kind of kid who would wish pain or agony or a bad back on my own mom but I sure do wish she was not quite so athletic. If she were just stiff enough that she would stand at the door and nod approvingly and say, "That's just fine, Jamie, just fine," I would have a lot more time to play on Saturdays.

Instead she comes bouncing in on her tennis shoes and stands on tiptoe to look at closet shelves and pulls drawers in and out and plops right down on her knees and looks under the bed.

Then back up she stands and I have to start hauling stuff out from under there.

Finally I had everything all out and sorted. There was a pile of trash, of course, and another big stack of dirty clothes. Then there were three library books that I'd already convinced the librarian had been stolen from my locker by some enemy of mine who wanted all of my allowance money to go to the Millard C. Fillmore Library Fund in fines.

I was sitting there staring at where I had piled up

all the really important things that I didn't know what to do with when the noise started outside.

It sounded like the gears of something screaming for help. My first thought was of Wally Parsons who races his car up and down our street all the time. He does it because he knows it ruins the street for us kids, and Wally is that kind of person who likes ruining things for other people.

But Wally's gears never grind. His tires squeal a lot, but I don't think gears grind when a car is going as fast as Wally Parsons drives his. And anyway, this gear noise had another sound along with it. The other noise was the kind you make in a grocery store when you run around an aisle too fast and catch your foot in the very bottom can of a whole pyramid-shaped display of tomato soup. And in with the grinding sound and the clattering and rolling tin sound was a sort of gasp like a motor with a bad case of the flu.

I got to my window fast enough to see a truck go by the house. You never saw a truck working that hard to get up a hill. It was clawing and gasping and spitting out black smoke behind itself. The cab of the truck was a sort of silver color, but the rest of the truck was all hidden under things that were tied on with wire and twine and something red and white with handles that looked like a jumping rope. There were bicycles and lamps and two sawhorses. There

11

were a lot of little leggy tables and a big playpen with a coil of fencing wire rolling around inside it. With all that stuff showing, I couldn't figure out what was packed inside the truck.

I knew it was worth the whole next week in play-time to leave that mess on the floor. I threw the clothes in the hamper and the books on my desk and all the rest in the trash. After all, I am young. Maybe I'll get another chance at a Texas license plate, a bunch of old spikes from a railroad, and a collection of candy-bar wrappers of every kind they sell down at Prescott's Five and Dime.

By that time the truck had made it to the trees that hide the driveway of the Owens place. I heard it shudder with relief and the motor cough weakly as it stopped up there.

The Owens house is at the very top of our hill. It is the kind of house that people move in and out of all the time. Sometimes they hardly stay long enough to find out whether they like it or not. It's kind of nice to have a house like that around because none of us kids who live on the street have ever moved and can't really imagine what moving is like. My mom laughed when I said that. "I would tell you, Jamie," she said, "but I know how poorly you sleep after horror stories."

Amy Morris had come out to see what the noise

was too. She was standing on her front steps with a sister by one hand and a brother by the other. Amy has the biggest family on our block. She even has the biggest family of any kid in the Millard C. Fillmore Elementary School. She may have the biggest family in the world, for all I know.

Amy is ten, and she has to help with all the smaller kids. That morning she had her sister E on her left side and her brother F on her right. She had to get them safely down on the sidewalk before she could stand and stare up the hill with me. All those kids look alike with kind of pale hair, and eyes like blue washers with black holes in the middle. She knows all their names but the rest of us just use their initials. After Amy there is Bradford, then Carrie, then Douglas. Then Eliza is next and about three now, I guess. Forrest is going on two and bawls an awful lot. I can't remember what the baby's name is but it begins with a G which is lucky enough for us.

"What's that awful clatter about?" Amy asked when she had Forrest's nose wiped with the tissue she always has in her pocket.

"A truck loaded up with all kinds of stuff just went up the hill to the Owens house," I told her.

"New people," she said, and then she sighed. My dad said that I might sigh a lot too if I never had a hand to call my own.

Edie Danvers came out to join us in her scared way. George Harvey almost knocked her down as he came running over. George always runs everywhere he goes. "Do you think they have a kid our age?" he asked.

He's always saying he wishes some more kids would move in around us so we could divide up and play running games. He knows he would win. He's not only the best runner on our block, he's also the fastest runner in the Millard C. Fillmore Elementary School. No one else is even close, except that skinny-legged Abbie with braces who usually comes in second. George claims he is the best runner in the whole world and is only waiting to be old enough for the Olympics so he can prove it and have his picture in the paper.

"It will probably be another big bully like that Wally Parsons who will come down that hill and beat up on us every day on the way to school," Edie Danvers warned.

Edie is a real worrier. She learned it from her folks. They worry when she plays with us boys because we are rough. Her mother even worries when Edie plays with Amy because E or F or someone might have a runny nose for Edie to catch. Not only is Edie the only world-class worrier but she also has the honor of having a baby sister who is the baldest kid in the world. Not just on our street or in our school but in the whole world. There isn't even the sign of a hair on that kid except for little skinny eyebrows that only show when the light is right.

"You're a worrywart," George scoffed at her. "How do you always manage to come up with such awful ideas?"

It *was* an awful idea. In fact it was a scary idea. Wally lives between our block and the Millard C. Fillmore School where we all go. For years there it was worth our lives to go down that street without watching all sides for him flying out at us. He used to catch worms and drop them in our hair if we walked under the trees. He scraped all the old bubble gum from under the tables at the ice cream shop and spread it on the hot cement so that we tracked big wads of pink dirt into school with us. He stretched wire across the backfield of the ball diamond in the park so that, if you backed up for a fly, you tripped and nearly broke your head on that old baked clay.

He's the only kid in the world who would freeze water balloons before he threw them at you. The teachers and the principal of the Millard C. Fillmore School had a big celebration party when Wally Parsons graduated from the eighth grade. They voted him Least Likely to be Missed, not just for that year but in the whole history of the school.

Now the only way he has to bully us is with his car and that is bad enough.

I was still thinking about having a bully move in at the Owens house when Zach Lund finally came out. Zach is always the last one to get anywhere. He's going to be an animal doctor when he grows up. In the meantime he practically has a zoo of his own. Every single morning before he leaves home he has to:

Feed his mice (3) and his pet rat.
Change the paper underneath his canary and give it seed.
Empty the cat box and put in new litter.
Brush and feed his dog and put him out in the yard.
Feed and water his pet gerbils (2) and his guinea pig (1).

He has been tardy so many mornings that Miss Button doesn't even bother to write it down. She makes a mark when he gets there on time and then subtracts it from how many days there were. For his next birthday he is going to get hermit crabs. He is sort of famous for all his animals because there isn't anybody in school that is even close except a boy named Buford whose father owns a farm. We don't count his father's pigs because Buford's parents plan to eat them when they get big enough.

Zach almost always has something alive in his pocket. That day he had a pet mouse. Edie stepped back really far from him when he lifted it out and began to stroke it between the ears with one finger the way he does. I was just going to tell him about the truck with all the stuff fastened on it when I felt a sudden hard nudge in my ribs.

"Wow," I heard George say in a low voice. "Will you look at that?"

The boy on the bike had come out of the trees that hide the driveway to the Owens house. He came fast and began to make big figure eights in the street with a wheelie at the curb on each side. The bike must have been green once because there were little spots of green in between the rusted places. The boy's hair was that off color that is pale at the ends but darker at the roots. It hung in his face so that you could barely see the end of his nose and little glints where his eyes looked out. Even from that distance you could see that his skin was a different shade from most boys' faces. He was dressed like anybody else—jeans with a patch and a T-shirt with some old washed-out lettering on it that I couldn't read—but his socks didn't match. He was wearing a green sock on his left foot and a brown sock on his right. And he was smiling as he came closer.

Then he made four wheelies, one right after the other there in the street by us and came to a stop.

"Hi," he said. "I'm Chester."

Edie is the one with the manners.

"Hi," she said right back. Then she pointed around at us.

"This is Amy, and Zach, and George, and Jamie. My name is Edie. Did you just move in up there today?"

He nodded and went on smiling. "Sure did. And boy, is it a mess! I just thought I'd take a break and look over the neighborhood."

"It's a nice neighborhood," Edie said primly. "We hope you like it, too."

"And the school is down there, just a block or two," George added helpfully.

"The Millard C. Fillmore Elementary," Zach added.

"That's good to know," Chester said, nodding and smiling.

I couldn't say anything. I could feel my tongue just stuck there in my mouth, dry and strange. Standing right by that boy I could see that Chester's face wasn't some strange color at all. Those were freckles. I hoped really hard that none of the other kids were looking at him as closely as I was.

You see, I have freckles too. I have the most

freckles of any kid on our block. In fact, I am famous all around school for having the most freckles of any kid by actual count. I have twenty-seven freckles on my face, which is more spots than Miss Button's Dalmation dog has all over. I looked at Chester's freckles and felt kind of sick. When you are used to being the most of something and it gets taken away from you, something you didn't even know was loose falls with a thud in the bottom of your stomach and just lies there.

My freckles are like chocolate chips in a cookie; there are light spaces in between. Chester's freckles were more like wheat cereal spilled out on a table. They were so close that there wasn't any space between them at all. Some of them looked like a freckle on a freckle, like you pile up checkers to make a king. The freckles across his nose were so close that I knew that if freckles could hold hands, that would be how they'd look.

George kept staring at Chester. Finally he whistled.

"Now those are what I call freckles," he said. You could tell how impressed he was by the way his voice rose.

George has always been jealous of me because he only has three freckles and one of them is on his eyelid which shouldn't even count because you can only see it plain when he is asleep.

"Yeah. Those are freckles all right," Chester said in that good-natured way, still smiling.

"How many freckles would you say you have, right off?" George asked.

I wanted to grind my foot right down on George's tennis shoe. What kind of a thing is it to have a freckle contest like that on a Saturday morning with a perfect stranger?

"Quite a few," Chester said.

"But exactly how many?" George pressed. All the other kids were staring now. Amy was standing on tiptoe to see so that little E and F were dangling by their arms. F began to howl and Amy lifted him up on her hip so he could see better.

"Forty-three," Chester replied. "But they're just freckles." Then he started pushing his pedals and began to make that circle with his bike again, no hands. He picked up speed, and did a huge wheelie, and grinned back at us. "Nice to meet you. I've got to go home and help put stuff away. See you around."

I could feel all those kids staring at me. I could see them subtracting my freckles (27) from Chester's freckles (43). I decided that I really hate the way people look when they are subtracting things in their heads. I hated George Harvey for being able to run faster than anybody and for asking Chester all those silly questions about freckles.

Come to think of it, I hated Chester and I didn't even know him.

"Come on, Jamie," Zach said quietly. "It's not the end of the world."

I acted as if I didn't even hear him and went back inside my own house.

Sunday

Some days just manage to have everything in the world wrong with them. That Sunday after Chester came was one of those days. Try as we would, us kids couldn't find anything we wanted to do.

We never are allowed to roller skate on Sunday because the people who aren't lucky enough to have kids all seem to want to sleep late in the morning or nap all afternoon.

It rained that Saturday night so the diamond over at the park was just one mud puddle after another. We don't dare play ball in the street because, the last time we tried, that Wally Parsons came roaring up the hill and almost caught Zach between second and third base with his fenders.

Finally we each put in a dime and walked over to the little grocery store by the park and bought a 49-cent ball of kite string and talked the man out of charging us tax. They always have leftover toys at Amy's house because they have so many birthdays. Amy found a kite somebody had given F and we got it all strung up and took turns. It was fun until George had to show off and run with it. Naturally he made it dive and it flopped into the top of a big cottonwood tree down at the far end of the block.

I was trying to boost Zach up into the tree when the man who owned the house there came out in his undershirt still carrying the sports pages of the Sunday paper.

I just held Zach up there while the man looked at the tree and our kite. Boy, was it ever quiet. There wasn't a sound anywhere except for the flopping of the kite high up when the wind hit it just right.

"If you please, sir," Edie began politely. "That's our kite and we are awfully sorry—"

The man didn't even let her finish. He only held up his hand and said, "Shhh . . . shhhhh," very firmly.

"Our friend could climb up there and get it down without breaking a single limb of your lovely tree," Edie whispered in this tiny little voice. "And if he should fall and be killed, none of us would press charges at all. We would all swear that it was not your fault no matter what happened."

24

He stared at her in astonishment, shrugged, and then said, "Be quiet, will you? I want to listen."

We all kind of cocked our ears but there still wasn't a sound from anywhere.

"I don't hear anything," Amy said suddenly. Even F, who had howled when she set him on the front steps to watch, had put his fingers in his mouth instead of yelling.

The man's face suddenly looked less intense. Then he began to smile and after a minute he was grinning like anything.

"Don't you hear it?" he asked. "That's silence, that's what it is. Beautiful, glorious silence. I have had starlings chattering and squawking in that tree for the last three weeks. I can't sleep for the starlings. I can't leave my car in the drive."

We looked over at the driveway. It was a gray driveway with white bird polka dots all over.

"And now they're gone. Every screaming one of them is gone. I thank you kindly, but you kids just scram on and mark this down as your good deed for the month."

"But the kite," Amy protested. "That's my brother's kite."

"Then your brother should have kept it out of my tree," the man told her.

"Just let us have the string back," I asked. There might be another old kite somewhere but we had paid good money for that string.

"Not on your life." The man shook his head. "For all I know, it was the string that scared them away."

We stood and stared at him a little while. He didn't even mind. He stared up at the tree looking contented and then went back into his house whistling.

We got out our skateboards and lined them up at the top of the hill. We were still arguing over how we could judge a race when Edie's father came out on the porch and waved us down there.

"Where were you thinking about riding those things?" he asked.

"Down the sidewalk," I told him. Everybody knows that we don't dare take them into the street since Wally Parsons got his driver's license.

I figured we were going to get a lecture about how dangerous skateboards are. He might even tell us about some gruesome accident where some boy's leg was broken so bad that it stuck right out through his sock. Edie's father is full of jolly blood stories like that. Instead he just shook his head and pointed at the paper he held in his hand.

"I hate to be the one to tell you kids this," he said in that voice grownups use when they don't hate it at all but know that you will. "The city just this week

26

passed an ordinance against the use of skateboards on public sidewalks. It seems that some kid ran into an old lady and by the time it was over they had to fasten her back with steel pins."

"But Daddy," Edie wailed. "We can't skateboard in the street because of Wally Parsons."

He sighed just like Edie always does. "I know, I know, Edie. I have been down to the police station five times now. The police are sympathetic to our problem but they have the law to consider. They can't do a thing about Wally Parsons' driving until they catch him in the act."

After Edie's dad went back in and we put the skateboards away, George grumbled, "Maybe we should draw straws and somebody volunteer to let Wally Parsons run over them. Then we'd have him."

"Whoever was left would have him," Zach corrected him, letting his guinea pig down to snuffle around in the grass.

"Draw," Amy said thoughtfully. "That's it. We can draw a hopscotch on a driveway." She went and got a piece of chalk from D's blackboard and we drew a big one on her driveway that went clear from the garage door to the sidewalk. We always make messes like that at Amy's house because, with all those kids, her folks are well past making a fuss about the way their house and yard look.

George went through first just to show off how fast he could do it. Amy went through next. I held onto E and F for her because Edie was afraid they might have a germ that would rub off on her hands and make her miss school. Zach was just starting his turn when George yelled,

"Hey, here comes Chester."

I didn't look around. I had already made up my mind that never in my whole life would I be friendly with anyone who had more freckles than I had. There was nothing personal about it, I told myself. I

would simply be known as a man who was not cordial to spotted people. Other than myself, of course.

But even from the corner of my eye I could see Chester flying down the hill on that once green bicycle with both arms folded over his chest and the wheelies getting bigger and bigger with every turn. He was wearing a blue-and-white sock on his right foot and a green one on his left. And he was smiling.

"Want to play?" George called. George is always looking for somebody new to beat at any game.

Chester made that last big circle on his bike and stopped right at the end of the drive. There was sweat on all of his forty-three freckles which made them look shiny like chocolate that the sun has shone on.

"Thanks a lot for asking me," Chester replied with that same grin. "I'd sure like to but we are going down

to look at the school and then look over the town."

"We?" Edie asked.

"Just my brothers and sisters and me," Chester answered, still smiling.

Then we saw them.

The whole top of that street was just nothing but bicycle wheels. It was like a Mongol invasion without horses. Colors spun in my head as I looked at the bikes, red and yellow and black and another green one like Chester's. At the very end of them all came a giant tricycle with one kid pedaling like mad and a smaller kid hanging onto the back. Every one of those bikes was being ridden by a kid with that off-colored hair, pale on the ends and darker at the roots where it grows out. They all had freckles. And they were all smiling.

Zach's dog began to bark from behind the fence. Then he began to run back and forth like crazy.

Chester stood there with us as they all whizzed by. They all waved at us because, except for the boy pedaling the tricycle, they all rode no hands. Even the kid on the trike grinned at us, showing a big dark place where her front teeth were missing.

"That is Jefferson," Chester told us.

"And Eleanor.

"And James.

"And Franklin with Angela riding on the back."

Zach's poor dog was about to bark his head off. His noise almost drowned out Chester's words, but we were all counting. Let's see, I told myself. Jefferson, Eleanor, James, Franklin, and Angela made five. Add one Chester and you have six kids.

Amy had been counting too. She had a strange flushed look on her face. You could tell she was pretty nervous. But there are seven kids in her family. When they all passed, she sighed the way Edie usually does and smiled happily.

"What a lovely thing it must be to have all those brothers and sisters," Edie said politely.

"Yeah," George agreed. "It's really great to see all your family." He was shouting over the barking of Zach's dog.

Chester's smile dropped for that one minute and he looked puzzled. Then he laughed. "Oh," he said. "But that's not *all* my family."

With that dog making so much noise I couldn't be sure I had heard him correctly.

"You mean there's more?" Zach shouted in a loud voice that made Amy shiver.

"There's just Sam and Uel," Chester said.

"What's a samanuel?" Edie asked in a careful voice as if she hoped it was not rude to ask.

Chester grinned even wider. "When the last baby was coming my parents had one awful time agreeing on a name they liked. They finally agreed on Samuel. There was nothing to do but split it in half when the baby was twins."

"Twins," Amy said in that tone of voice you use when you are telling a ghost story.

"But they're just babies," Chester said. Then he wheeled his bike in that circle with no hands and grinned back at us. "Thanks for asking me. I got to get along. See you around."

I didn't mean to do it but I realized that I was staring at Amy just the way the other kids were. She turned a slow red that went clear from the neck of her shirt to where her forehead was hidden under her bangs. Then she picked up the chalk and took her little brother and sister by the hand and started up the steps into the house.

"It's not the end of the world," Zach called after her—yelled, I should say, because his dog had gotten so excited that he was running circles in the yard, yelping.

Amy didn't answer. Instead she slammed the door so hard that the shutters on the house chattered like skeleton teeth.

Monday

When a new kid comes into your room at the Millard C. Fillmore Elementary School, he always comes in late. When the first hour of school passed and Chester was not brought to the door of our room by the principal, my hopes began to rise. Maybe they would put him in one of the other classes. Maybe he had been given to Mr. Grauer, who was in charge of the room right across the hall from ours. Maybe he was older or younger than the rest of us. After all, nobody had even thought to ask him, what with the wheelies and the freckle contest and the wheeled Mongol invasion.

But no. About half an hour before time for recess, there was Chester at the door, grinning that way he does, and Miss Button rising to greet him with a smile.

After she introduced him to the class, she looked around the room thoughtfully.

"We may have to use an extra large chair for you, Chester," she apologized. "I think all the ones this size are already in use."

There was George with his hand up first and his fingers snapping like a whip.

"I know where the chairs are in the storeroom," he volunteered. "Me and Zach could go get one in just a minute."

"Zach and I," she corrected, without even thinking. "That would be very nice of you, George."

I looked over at Amy. She covered her mouth with her hand and made a choking gesture as if she were going to lose her breakfast. I grinned and nodded at her. It was just plain sickening the way George and Zach had jumped up and zoomed out of there to show off their friendship with Chester. We knew about Chester, Amy and I did, him with his forty-three freckles and eight kids in his family, even if two of them only had half a name apiece.

Naturally it was Edie who jumped up to open the door for George and Zach when they came back with the chair—a big ugly chair for big ugly Chester whose socks probably didn't match. He had brand new jeans on that were longer than the patched ones he had worn over the weekend. They were folded at least twice, and still they hung down and covered his socks.

34

There was one nice thing about that chair being so big. Miss Button had it put clear at the back of the room so normal-sized people wouldn't have to peer around it. I sit up in front by the window so I wouldn't have to see Chester unless I wanted to turn around.

The bell rang just as the chair was all settled in, and we all went outside for recess. Wouldn't you know that, when we lined up, I would be there between George and Chester?

Mr. Allen is in charge of our recess. He is a big show-off who wears those sweat suits with stripes down the legs and tennis shoes with multicolored stripes on them. He wears this big whistle around his neck and bounces a ball with his left hand without looking at it. He chatters all the time and, since he doesn't have very much to say, he usually says the same thing over and over like a mynah bird.

"Line up, line up, line up there," he was chattering. "Quick race here today, just a quick race. Winners of the race will choose the teams for today's game."

I heard George say "Yeah," under his breath. Mr. Allen always chooses captains that way and George always gets to be a captain because he is the fastest runner. The only time I ever won one of those races and got to be captain was when George broke a shoe-

35

lace and fell on his face and Abbie with the braces was home with a cold.

When Chester bent down to roll up his jeans for the race, I saw that he was wearing a plaid sock on his right foot and a green sock on his left. George was staring at his socks, too.

"How come you never wear socks the same color?" George asked curiously.

"It's just a system I worked out," Chester ex-

plained, still bent over folding those stiff new jeans.

The kids were all leaning forward to stare the way they do when anyone new is around. You could tell they were listening for his answer. I wasn't about to try to listen but a fellow can't help hearing if he's standing that close.

"What kind of a system do you mean?" George asked.

"Well." Chester pushed that off-color hair out of his eyes so that everybody could see he had freckles on his freckles clear up to where his hair started.

Then he stuck his left foot out and showed it to George. "I always wear green on that foot because I'm left-footed."

The kids looked around at each other and then back at Chester. Boy, some people really know how to get the spotlight and hold it.

"Left-footed?" George repeated like a question, just egging him on.

Chester nodded with that big smile of his. "Now, my brother Jefferson is left-handed and left-footed both. Eleanor is right-handed but left-footed. James and Franklin are right-handed and right-footed all the way." He paused. "We don't know about the twins yet but I am right-handed and left-footed like Eleanor."

George looked more confused than ever.

"What has all that got to do with your socks?" he asked.

"It's really pretty simple," Chester explained. "If a left-footed person starts out running on his right foot, he'll get off to a slow start. Just like if a right-footed person should try to start on his left foot. I always wear a green sock on my left foot to remind myself that green is for *Go*."

Just as Chester said *Go*, Mr. Allen tooted that whistle of his again.

"All right, all right, all right," he shouted, still

bouncing that ball. "The race is to the fence and back. The first two to make it to the fence will be the captains of the kickball teams for today."

When Mr. Allen whistled the next time, everybody crouched over to get a sprinting start.

I heard George say "Yeah" again, that satisfied way, almost under his breath.

"Ready?" Mr. Allen shouted, dancing off to the side with the whistle bouncing on his chest.

The whole line of kids was in position, each with one foot forward and leaning over with arms bent like chicken wings.

Then I noticed George. He was staring at his right foot sticking out in front of him. Then he glanced over at Chester, whose left foot, in that bright green sock, was stuck out in front. George pulled his right foot in and put his left foot out the way Chester had his. Then he shook his head and started to change his feet again just as Mr. Allen blew the whistle and shouted, "*Go!*"

That Chester went off flying. All the rest of us were pumping across the yard as fast as we could go. Everybody was pushing against the line that sort of stayed together crossing the school yard, except for Chester who was way out in front from the very first minute. And George.

I guess that *Go* whistle must have blown when

George was halfway through changing his feet again. Anyway, he lost his balance and fell down flat in the dirt with all our dust blowing in his face.

He was up right away of course, but it was too late.

Chester came in first. That Abbie with the braces and the long skinny legs like a stork came in second.

"Well, well, well," Mr. Allen said. "So somebody has come along who can beat George Harvey."

The whole class looked at George. George had been the fastest runner in our room since we started out together in kindergarten. When they had all-school field days, George had even beaten some of the eighth-grade runners.

Abbie picked George for her team right off. George scowled and dragged his feet, going over to stand in the line behind her. Chester just stood there grinning that way he does with that green sock shining like a *Go* sign on his left foot.

"That was a dirty filthy rotten trick," George mumbled as Zach took the place in line behind him.

I looked around for Amy. When I caught her eye, I winked at her.

She grinned at me from ear to ear. "I would wink back, Jamie," she whispered. "But I just can't decide whether I am right- or left-eyed."

Tuesday

During all these years that the five of us have lived on this street together and been friends, we have never taken sides against each other. Sometimes George and I have gotten into it because he is such a big head. Once Amy and Edie didn't speak for a whole week after one of Amy's little brothers gave Edie the chicken pox and she had to miss the Millard C. Fillmore School Field Day because of quarantine. Zach was really mad at me one summer when I accidentally killed his pet rat, Hector. I was sorry enough, but how is a fellow to know that a rat is sleeping under the cushions of a porch swing?

But after Chester came, by Tuesday we were two groups instead of just one. We went home together like that, George and Amy and I up front and Zach and Edie trailing behind.

Every few minutes Zach would stop and get off his

41

bike and do something on the ground. I really wanted to know what he was doing but I wasn't about to talk to him, not after the things he and Edie kept saying to us.

"Jealous, that's all you are," Edie said in the tone of voice of somebody who knows everything in the whole world. "Each one of you is jealous of Chester. So what if he has twice as many freckles as you do, Jamie? It's not that big a deal."

"Boy, I don't know how you ever get through arithmetic," I scoffed at her. "Twice as many freckles. I guess that two times twenty-seven is all of a sudden forty-three."

"So what's eleven freckles more or less when somebody has as many as Chester has?" Edie asked breezily. "And you, Amy, that's so silly. There's only one more in his family than you have, but I bet from the looks of his brothers and sisters that his parents started sooner."

"At least we give all of our kids whole names," Amy said grumpily. "Sam and Uel. Silly."

"I guess you're going to light into me because I didn't like being tricked into losing that race," George told her. "You might just as well save your breath. I know a dirty rotten trick when I see one, and I'm not obliged to like it, either."

Zach was down on the ground pinching at something so that his voice came muffled. "You're either the fastest runner or you're not," he told George. "You might as well be a good sport about it. It's not the end of the world, you know."

That was when I finally figured out that Zach was filling his shirt pocket with that little white fluff that blows off the cottonwood trees.

"What are you doing?" Amy asked him in an irritated voice. "What do you want all that white stuff for anyway?"

"My white rat is building a nest," Zach explained. "She likes soft stuff like this to line it."

"Well, that ought to make a seedy bunch of little rats," George scoffed. "Zach's zoo."

"Well, keeping a zoo isn't something you win at one day and lose the next," Zach told him.

George stopped in his tracks. "I could hit you for saying stuff like that," he warned.

"I couldn't probably run away before you caught me," Zach replied with a grin.

George let out a big growl and jumped off his bike. Edie started to squeal the way she always does when it looks like somebody might hit somebody else. George and Zach might have really had a fight if a larger, louder squeal hadn't sounded at the same minute, drowning out Edie's little noise.

The squeal was tires. The blue sedan that Wally

Parsons drives came roaring up the hill as if it were jet propelled. You could see Wally crouching there behind the wheel with that mean look he gets when he is trying to hurt somebody. The car swerved toward us for all the world as if it meant to make a big wheelie right on top of us. It was headed toward us so straight that I thought I could see the little bulbs inside the headlights.

You never saw kids move so fast. Bicycles and books and coats came flying out of that street into one big crashing heap on the sidewalk. We barely made it before that car went roaring on by, leaving the air filled with that bad stink from no-lead gas and a whole cloud of cottonwood fluff that had flown out of Zach's pocket.

"Wow." Zach let his air out heavily. "What if somebody's pet dog had been out in that street?"

"Or a brother or a sister?" Amy asked in a kind of weak voice.

"Never mind the dogs and babies," Edie wailed. "What if *we* hadn't made it? I don't want to be all crushed and hurt and killed by that awful old car. I wish the policemen would just go and arrest Wally Parsons and take his permit to drive away from him like my dad keeps telling them to."

"My dad has talked to the police too," I told her.

"They keep saying that they have to catch him in reckless driving. They have a whole stack of complaints but mostly they are from little kids like us."

"Kids are breakable, too," Zach grumbled. "And look at my bike."

"That's the way to be a hero around here," George agreed. "Just move slow and help put Wally Parsons away." He and Zach both tugged at their bikes which had gotten tangled in the rush of throwing them to safety.

We were all so busy trying to get that mess straightened out that we didn't even see Chester until he stopped his bike in the street beside us.

"Got a problem?" he asked.

"We nearly got run over by a madman," Zach explained, finally getting his bike free. Chester leaned over and hit the side of his hand against the hood of the back wheel where it was all bent out at a funny angle. George and Amy and I just stood there.

"Well," Chester said, still helping. "Who was the fast one who got his bicycle on the bottom of the heap?"

I heard George's little growl even as Edie replied, "Mine. Oh, my gosh, look at it."

Chester was right. Her bike had been at the very bottom of the pile. With the others lifted off, you could see that some of her spokes were really badly bent and the little red disc inside her backlight was shattered on the grass.

"You shouldn't try to ride it like that," Chester told her, poking at the spokes with his finger.

"It's never going to be the same again," Edie wailed. "My beautiful bike!"

"Sure it will be the same," Chester told her calmly. "I bet your dad can use a pair of pliers on this and have it ready by school time tomorrow. If I had the right pliers, I could do it myself, right here. The light will be something extra," he added. "You'll have to buy a new one of those."

Edie really tuned up. For once she had something real to worry about. "Maybe it won't ride the same," she wailed. "What if it rusts?"

"It'll be okay," Chester assured her. "And as for rust, it weighs the same as paint. It doesn't slow a bike down."

When his words didn't help, Chester's voice dropped to a kind of coaxing. "Hey," he said. "I'll tell you what. You take my bike and ride it home and I'll wheel yours along for you. Then your dad will fix it tonight. I just bet he will."

Edie was startled into silence. Since she has such good manners, the rest of us never have to worry about ours. But here was Chester being polite and thoughtful and helpful all at once. She stared at him a minute. Then her face turned all pink and she said, "Thank you ever so much, Chester," in the sickliest little voice you ever heard.

"Oh, it's just a little hill," Chester said, handing her his handlebars.

George and Amy and I wheeled on ahead. Amy made that getting-sick motion with her hand over her mouth again and I nodded because I thought that had been a pretty sloppy scene myself. But we did hang back going up the hill so we could hear what they were talking about.

Edie asked Chester how he liked his new house.

He said pretty well except that the roof leaked in his sister's room and they still hadn't had time to get a fence built around the yard.

Edie asked him what he thought of the Millard C. Fillmore Elementary School.

He said he liked it pretty well so far except that he was way ahead of us in geography and way behind in arithmetic.

Edie's mother always watches from the window to see that Edie gets home on time and all in one piece. She must have seen us coming from clear down the street. When we got there, she was standing on the front porch with a worried frown, holding Edie's baby sister in her arms.

"Are you all right, Edith?" she called before we even reached the house. "Why aren't you riding your own bicycle? I know something is wrong, dear. Don't hide things from Mother."

"I'm fine, Mom," Edie shouted a couple of times. Then, when we were all right there at the porch, she explained to her mother.

"I got some bent spokes in my wheel and Chester kindly asked me to ride his bike home."

Her mother was still frowning when Edie remembered.

"Oh, Mom, this is Chester who just moved in with his family at the Owens house. Chester, this is my mom."

Chester had wheeled the bike right up on the porch. He fixed the kickstand and wiped his palm on his pants and reached out to shake hands. Then he noticed the baby and his grin got even wider.

"Hey," he said with delight. "Is that your new baby?"

"She's the only one we've ever had," Edie told him. Then she must have remembered that Chester didn't know that she had the baldest baby in the world for her very own. You could see Edie swell with pride as Chester grinned at the baby. You could see her just waiting for him to notice how perfectly hairless that

baby was without a single bit of fuzz on it anywhere except for those stingy little eyebrows.

One thing I have to give Chester. He sure knows how to look at babies. I always just stare at them and can't think of anything to say that wouldn't be either silly or an out-and-out lie. But of course he has had more experience at looking at babies than I have. He nodded and made a clucky noise and grinned. Then he turned the blanket back and looked at the baby's fat arm.

"Wow," he said in this really impressed tone. "That is one pretty baby. And look at that smile."

Edie's mother kind of glowed and held the baby up a little more so that Chester could admire her. "That's probably only gas bubbles," she said. "She's really too young to smile."

But Edie wasn't as tickled as her mother obviously was. In fact, she was getting that worried look back on her face.

"But she's bald," Edie pointed out to Chester. "Look at that. She's absolutely perfectly bald. She doesn't have a single shred of hair anywhere on her, except for eyebrows."

Clear from the street you could see the sun shining on that baby's head. Its head gleamed so much in the light that I could feel my eyes begin to water from the brightness. I wondered if Edie's mother hadn't actually polished the baby's head to make it so naked and shiny. Even Chester would have to admit that Edie's baby was as bald as a pink rock.

"We say that she is the baldest baby in the whole entire world," Edie announced proudly. But her voice sounded a little frantic. She was used to having absolute strangers stop the buggy and talk about the baby's head, and here Chester was just taking it as a matter of course.

Chester grinned over at Edie in that relaxed way of his.

"I wouldn't worry about your baby being bald, Edie," he said in that pleasant way. "Both my little twin brothers, Sam and Uel, are bald."

"No hair at all?" Edie asked, her face getting a little gray.

"Not a sign," Chester said, shaking his head. "Not a single sign of hair."

"But they do have eyebrows?" Edie pressed, getting a little desperate.

Chester just looked astonished. "Sam and Uel? Oh, no. Neither of them has even a sign of an eyebrow, not even a little pink line that would show where eyebrows meant to come in."

Edie stared at him, trying to get used to having her

51

only claim to fame destroyed twice in the same family. I knew how she felt, and Amy knew and George knew, but it didn't help Edie in that awful moment.

Chester didn't seem to notice anything. In fact, he kind of laughed. "They aren't anything like as pretty as your baby is, Edie. Not only do they not have nice, well-shaped eyebrows like your baby, but they are all polka-dotted all over."

"Polka-dotted?" Edie's mom almost shrieked the word and grabbed her baby back against her chest.

"Oh, it's nothing that anyone can catch," Chester assured her. "They just get those spots because they are allergic to cow's milk and just about anything else Mom tries to feed them."

He was down the steps now and getting onto his own bike. "Nice to have met you," he told Edie's mom. "And I just bet your dad can fix that bike before supper even," he assured Edie. "See you around."

Then he went on up the hill in those wide circles, with the wheelies and everything.

Edie stared after him. First she whispered, "No eyebrows," under her breath. Then she said, "Polka dots," in a slightly higher tone.

All of us just waited there. Only Zach didn't understand.

"It's not the end of the world," he started to re-mind her, but she wouldn't even let him get the words out.

"Go back to your zoo," she shouted, and slammed the door right in his face.

Wednesday

Chester was right about Edie's dad being able to fix her bike. It looked as good as new when she rolled it out to ride to school the next morning. We all got out there about the same time, except for Zach. Since he is always late, we didn't wait around for him.

It had rained in the night and there was still a little spatter in the air when it was time to go. Mom made me wear that silly hat and raincoat she got me. It is some color of yellow that you wouldn't believe. She claims the color is for safety. I claim it simply makes me an easier target.

Anyway the hat is awful. It peaks down so that I can only see a little bit in front and hardly anything at the sides.

When we got to the crossing light by the school, it was on red. We were all clumped together there by our bikes watching for the light to change.

I know I would have seen that car coming if I hadn't had that silly yellow hat on. As it was, it was Edie who saw it and gave a big yell as she jumped back from the curb.

Who else but Wally Parsons? He had the right-of-way but, instead of staying in his lane, he swerved the car clear over to the curb where we were standing. His wheels roared through a big icky puddle. We were all splashed from head to toe with a mixture of water and mud that looked like one of those "cocoa" milk shakes they make at the ice cream store.

Amy gasped and Edie screamed. George said something that would have cost me a week's allowance at my house.

"That Wally Parsons," I yelled, shaking my fist after the car. "I hope that gutter is full of nails and he gets four flat tires all at once."

"Where there are bears," Amy added.

I stared at her. "There aren't any bears around here," George told her in a funny mushy voice. He had mud even in his mouth.

"I am wishing bears," Amy said in a low, furious voice.

Edie fished in her raincoat pocket and handed paper hankerchiefs all around. Her mother always sends her with twice as many as she needs, which was about half as many as we all needed. After we used them up, we went into class all smeared instead of with the full mud masks which we would have had without them.

Miss Button gasped a little when we all walked in, but she went ahead and took the roll and collected lunch money before sending all of us to the washrooms to clean some more of the mud off.

I was the first one back because of that big yellow coat and hat. Edie was the last one back because she takes dirt more seriously than the rest of us do. You could tell it was really late because Zach was there in his seat when I went in.

I saw Miss Button frowning at the back of the room. I looked around and saw that big ugly chair of Chester's sitting there empty. I saw her put a mark in her rollbook before she started class.

First we handed in papers. As they were laid on her desk Miss Button looked up brightly. "Wasn't it fun to write an interesting story about something that really happened to you?"

"No," the class answered in one solemn chorus.

"Now come on." She smiled winningly. "It must have been a teeny weeny bit of fun."

Everybody wriggled in their seats and looked at each other. The answer was still "No." It had been awful. I'd finally decided to write about a camping trip we took to Canada.

It had rained almost the whole time and our clothes smelled like mold. When it finally stopped raining the air was so full of mosquitoes that you had to breathe in through a net unless you wanted even your tonsils bitten. Mom couldn't get a fire to burn with wet wood so we ate things out of the can. Finally Mom began to cry and Dad took us to a motel so she could have a nice hot shower. It was cold in my room so I took the blankets off the bed and curled up in the closet where there wasn't any draft. In the morning they thought I was kidnapped and had policemen stamping all over the place before I woke up and was found.

And they were just regular policemen, not Mounties in red coats with horses or anything. I got so bored writing the story that I even went to sleep trying to copy it over.

Miss Button kept on asking us questions, trying to get some volunteers to say that they had just loved the assignment, when I heard the floor squeak.

I looked around and there was Chester trying to sneak in quietly on his tiptoes. With him up on his toes like that, I could see that he had a bright yellow sock on his right foot and a green one on his left. He was carrying his hat upside down but it still dripped on the floor.

When Miss Button caught his eye, he smiled at her and said, "I am sorry to be late. I really am."

She smiled back at him and I wondered what had gotten into that woman. How could she like Chester so well when none of us kids on our block could stand him except Zach?

"I am sure you have a good reason for being so late," she said in a soothing tone as he sat down.

He nodded soberly. "Yes, ma'am, I believe I do."

She looked around the room at all of us with a sort of exasperated look. "This entire class has been trying to tell me that nothing interesting has happened in their whole lives. I think they simply are not trying. Would you say that an 'interesting experience' made you late this morning?"

Chester frowned a moment before answering. "It was interesting to me," he admitted.

"Very well." She drew her lips tight for a moment and nodded her head. "Now, class, we will hear an interesting experience from Chester that will explain why he was"—she stopped and checked her watch—"twenty-two-and-a-half minutes late for class."

She waited as Chester just stood there, smiling.

"You may begin," she said after a moment.

Chester shuffled his feet and coughed. It looked as if he was trying to think of a title. What he finally announced was simple enough.

"Why I Was Twenty-two-and-a-half Minutes Late to Class."

I caught Amy's eye and she shrugged. George was glowering at Chester from his seat, and even Edie was staring off into space as if she would refuse to find anything interesting in his talk even if it had fireworks and bears in it. (Edie is just about equally scared of both those things.) Only Zach was looking at Chester eagerly. But then, Zach is a specialist at being late and had more interest in the story than the rest of us.

"It rained last night," Chester began. "Whenever it rains in our house, the roof leaks. The water always drips into my sister Eleanor's room. This morning it came in a big stream and got my sister's budgie all wet."

Miss Button leaned forward and interrupted. "Budgie?" she asked.

"Yes, ma'am," Chester replied. "That's her little green bird that looks something like a parrot and talks."

We all looked at Zach. Zach has a canary called Twit. He isn't called Twit because he makes that sound but because he never makes any sound at all. He doesn't even squeak. The closest he comes to making a sound is when he throws seeds out on the floor.

But Chester was not through.

"When my sister took her budgie out of the cage to

get him dried off, the budgie got away from her. It started to fly around the kitchen, and my sister Angela's Manx started after it."

"Her what?" Miss Button asked.

"Manx," Chester replied. "That is some kind of a cat that comes from an island somewhere and hasn't any tail at all."

He looked at Miss Button but she just nodded and motioned for him to go on.

"Whenever that Manx starts to run around it gets my brother Jefferson's dog all excited. He's a dingo, you see, and gets excited very easily."

"Who is a dingo, Chester?" Miss Button asked.

"The dog," Chester replied. "He's really from a kind of wild dog and came from Australia. He has spots all over. Like the twins."

"So the budgie is flying around the kitchen being chased by a cat with no tail, and the spotted dingo is chasing the Manx," Miss Button recited as if she wanted to be sure she had it all straight.

Chester nodded. "That's right. And that was how the fishbowl got knocked over. My mother is terribly afraid of those fish that my brother James keeps, so she grabbed both the babies and ran outside."

"Why is your mother so afraid of your brother's fish?" Miss Button asked, with a slightly glazed expression on her face.

"They are piranhas," Chester explained with that bland smile. "They come from South America and they like strange things to eat. Ever since Mom saw them eat a whole hamburger in a split second, she has just been really scared of them."

"Of course," Miss Button agreed, leaning back weakly. "I have to say that was an interesting reason for you to be twenty-two-and-a-half minutes late for class."

Chester looked astonished. "But, ma'am," he said in that soft polite tone. "That isn't all. You see when Mom ran out with the twins, the Manx cat ran along with her and the dingo ran the cat up the tree and it wouldn't come down."

"So you had to climb the tree and get your sister's cat down," Miss Button guessed.

"Not exactly," Chester said. "That isn't the kind of a tree that anyone could climb. Mom called the fire-truck and we had to wait for them to come with their tall ladder. But when the firetruck came, Tui wouldn't let the firemen get off the truck until I tied her up."

"Now who is Tui?" Miss Button asked in that sort of tired voice as if she wished she had given him an excused tardy in the first place.

"She is our family goat," Chester explained. "Only she doesn't know she is a goat. She has always run

with the dingo so she thinks she is a dog like him. She thinks she is the family watchdog. In fact, she even sometimes chases cars."

"And whose pet is Tui?" Miss Button asked.

Chester was thoughtful for a moment. "I guess you might say she belongs to the twins, Sam and Uel. We only got her because they have those spots all over."

Chester stopped and just stood there smiling. Miss Button nodded her head and looked off into the corner of the room thoughtfully.

The rest of us kids all looked at Zach.

So Chester's family had a budgie that talked, a cat with no tail from an island, a wild spotted dog from Australia, fish from South America that ate hamburgers, and a goat that chased cars. Zach just sank down in his seat, like one of those hermit crabs he wants scooting backward into a shell.

When Miss Button finally found her voice, she asked, "Chester, did you bring your essay to hand in?"

Chester flushed. The freckles all disappeared in a

great rush of red to his face. "I'm really sorry, ma'am. In all the excitement this morning, I somehow left it at home."

Miss Button smiled. "With the agreement of the class, I will accept your story of being late as an oral essay that shows an interesting experience." She glanced around the room. "What do you say, class? Is that all right with you?"

There was a great roar of approval from all the kids who don't live on our block. The only people who didn't shout "Yes" or stamp or whistle were Amy and Edie and George and Zach and me.

"Do give my best wishes to your mother, Chester," Miss Button said quietly as the room began to settle down again.

Thursday

"If anyone tells me that it is not the end of the world, I will hit him in the mouth," Zach said quietly.

None of us said anything. It was after school and we were all sitting on the back steps at Amy's house just staring. For once Amy didn't even have any kids hanging onto her. She had agreed to divide a whole week's allowance between Bradford and Carrie if they promised to take care of Douglas and Forrest and Eliza for her.

"I'm feeling really down," Edie admitted. "I worry when I feel like this. Do you suppose that an ordinary girl like me would know that the world was coming to an end by the way she felt? It could be, you know. The world could be coming to an end. It could be the end of the . . ."

"Don't say that," Zach groaned. "Just don't talk about it at all."

65

Zach had his dark-brown guinea pig in his jacket pocket. He took it out and handed it to Edie. "Just stroke him with your finger gently," he told her. "It will make you feel a lot better. He doesn't have spots or eat hamburger or chase cars but he sure feels good to stroke."

"How could one kid do that to every single one of us?" George asked. "We were so special. Every kid in school always said that we had the most special neighborhood in the whole Millard C. Fillmore School District, if not the world. How could one kid with a grin like a ninny and socks that don't match make us feel like five nothings?"

"It *is* the end of the world," Zach announced suddenly. "The way I can tell that it is the end of the world is that now I don't even care whether I get hermit crabs for my birthday or not."

None of us argued with him.

Maybe in the beginning it had been a kind of joke that there was something special about each one of us—the most freckles, the most kids in the family, the fastest runner, the baldest baby, and the greatest home zoo.

But somewhere along the line it quit being a joke. Everybody deep down inside wants to be the best of something, even if it isn't anything really important.

Nobody wants to be second best. Nobody wants to be a loser.

Suddenly someone coughed.

"Bless you," Edie said dully without even looking up.

"That wasn't a sneeze, it was a cough," a strange voice said. "I was just trying to get your attention."

We all looked up. There above the top of Edie's fence was a head of that off-color hair that was darker underneath and pale at the ends. There was a nose with freckles running all the way across it and over onto the cheeks. That could have been Chester himself except that the hair was pulled back and tied with a plaid ribbon and the face wasn't smiling.

"I'm Eleanor," the girl explained. "I'm Chester's sister and I am looking for a goat."

We all got up and went over to the fence.

"We don't have a goat," Amy told her, because it was Amy's yard. B and C had stopped pushing the swings and right away Forrest set up this big howl.

"Push," Amy shouted at them. "Push or you don't get any money."

The creak of the swings started up again and Amy turned back to the fence.

"I'm not looking for just any goat," Eleanor explained. Now she was smiling that same gentle way that Chester does. "I am looking for our own goat, whose name is Tui."

"Did he run away?" George asked.

"Oh, gracious no." Eleanor looked as if she were astonished at the idea. "Tui never runs except when she is chasing cars. She probably just ate through her rope and walked away. We haven't had a chance to put her fence up yet."

Amy pushed the gate open but Eleanor stayed out-

side as if she were a little shy. She was not so tall as Chester but just as slender and strong looking. She was wearing jeans with patches on the knees and a shirt with the sleeves rolled up almost to her elbows. The shirt was blue and so were her socks, both of them. Maybe she wasn't into running, I thought.

I just kept looking at her while she talked with Amy and the others. She was nice to look at. Her freckles were not quite as dark as Chester's nor as

thick and reddish as mine. For a girl who was taller than I and had a whole faceful of freckles like that, she sure managed to look pretty.

"We'll help you look for your goat," I offered. "We weren't doing anything else anyway."

She smiled right at me, not that steady, ready smile like Chester's but a sort of surprised and delighted smile. I have to say that I am that kind of kid who really likes to be smiled at personal like that.

"That would be swell," she said. "Chester and Jefferson and James and Franklin are all out looking but none of us has had any luck yet."

"How about Angela and Sam and Uel?" Amy asked in a kind of strained voice.

"Oh, they are too little to leave the yard," Eleanor said.

"Where does a goat go when it runs . . . walks away, I mean?" George asked.

"Tui would go just about anywhere she hadn't been before," Eleanor explained. "She is a very curious goat and she likes to look at new things."

"I am not sure I wouldn't be afraid of a goat," Edie said thoughtfully.

Eleanor frowned at her. "Actually there is a trick to managing goats. Just never turn your back on one. Face to face, they behave quite nicely."

I wanted Eleanor to smile at me again so I spoke up.

"How about we organize a Great Goat Hunt?" I asked. "We could all fan out and search in different directions. We could cover most of this part of town in nothing flat. And we do have the advantage of knowing our way around."

"What about me?" Amy wailed.

"You could be the Captain of the search," I decided out loud. "This yard could be headquarters. We would all check in for instructions from you. You could make a map of the area and mark off all the places that have already been searched."

"Oh, that would be very valuable when you are searching for a moving target," George said acidly. He always uses that tone of voice when anyone except himself takes charge of anything.

"George, could I go along with you?" Edie asked very quietly. "I would be afraid to find the goat by myself but I could help you."

He told her "Sure," in that big kind of voice that shows that he was flattered to have her ask.

That left me and Zach to go off and search together. Amy found a jumping rope with one handle gone and cut it in half so each team would have a leash to lead the goat back.

71

"Just hand her some grass, tell her she's beautiful, and tie the rope around her collar," Eleanor instructed us. "After a handful of grass that she didn't have to pluck herself she will follow you anywhere."

Zach and I were only halfway down the block when he turned and spoke to me firmly.

"I just want it understood that I am not going on this Goat Hunt for Chester. It is just that this may be the only Goat Hunt I ever have a chance at and I would be silly to miss an opportunity like this."

I wasn't doing it for Chester either but I didn't want to tell Zach that, so I kidded him.

"I think you owe it to yourself to go," I told him in a serious tone of voice. "Who knows how it will all end? I can see the headlines now—FAMOUS VETERINARIAN PLUNGED TO FIRST FAME IN DRAMATIC GOAT SEARCH."

"You don't plunge to fame, silly," he said crossly. "You rise to fame."

"Maybe the goat Tui is trapped in a deep hole," I told him. "But have it your way. It's your fame, not mine."

Only after we were well on our way did I realize how poorly I was prepared for the hunt. I had never seen this goat.

"Do goats come in all colors?" I asked Zach.

"Not all colors," he said. "They don't come in red or orange or green or purple . . ."

"Stop that," I told him. "I mean, what will it look like?"

"Brown or black or white or yellow," he decided. "Or any combination of those colors. I guess we could have asked Eleanor."

He wasn't any help. I tried to remember back to when I had seen the goats at the children's zoo. They had been tiny, just a little taller than my knee, and most of them had been black and white except one brown one that had taken my bandanna out of my pocket and started eating it while I was petting another goat.

Zach and I walked all the way down our street and then turned right and went up Roosevelt to where the houses ended and businesses started. We looked behind hedges and garages and along the alleys that we passed. Whenever we heard a dog barking we went to see if it was Tui that it was barking at.

At first we asked a lot of people if they had seen a loose goat. Nobody had seen a goat but everyone had some sort of joke to make about "old goats" and "lost kids" and had we tried down at the cannery?

I really expected the search to be over by the time we checked back with Amy, but she just shook her head and made a mark on her chart of the blocks we had searched.

The next time we went over by the tracks where the commuter trains were beginning to come in because it was getting near suppertime.

We saw two alley cats having a fight and a man in a three-piece business suit fixing a bicycle. We found a quarter in the dirt that somebody had dropped at the bus stop but no sign of a goat anywhere.

We both saw the quarter at the same time. We decided that Zach could have thirteen cents and I could have twelve because he got his hand down on it faster.

The next time we checked in with Amy, I asked about Eleanor.

"She's been by a couple of times just like you have," Amy told me. Then she showed me all the places that had been searched. "No luck anywhere so far."

"I have to go in when the street lights go on," Edie reminded us as she and George came up. George was still carrying his piece of rope with no goat on its end.

Just as if by magic the street lights went on along the block. The light came on at Edie's house at the same moment.

"Maybe we better all check in at home," Zach suggested, with a glance at his own front porch. "If we don't tell our folks where we are, we will have people looking for people looking for a goat."

Mom said I had to eat supper before I could return to the Great Goat Hunt.

"How could anyone lose a goat, anyway?" Mom asked as she served my plate. She put a big gob of something green on it.

I hate everything in the world that is green. I hate broccoli and Brussels sprouts and green beans, and spinach probably most of all. I hated green long before I ever heard of anyone named Chester with a green sock on his left foot. The kids will tell you that I always give away my green jelly beans without even asking for a trade for them. I hate them that much. So there was broccoli being heaped on my plate, turning the edges of my corn green and leaking around looking for something else to stain.

"They haven't had time to put a fence in yet, so the goat just ate through her rope and walked off," I explained.

"But why do they have a goat at all?" Dad asked, salting his potatoes before he even tasted them which always makes Mom mad.

"Because cow's milk makes spots on the babies," I told him.

"Babies?" Mom asked.

"They have two of them," I told her. "Twin boys."

I finished my corn and pushed the broccoli around in my gravy to make it look mostly eaten.

"I somehow got the idea that you weren't terribly fond of this new boy, Chester," Dad said as I folded my napkin by my plate.

"You don't have to like Chester to know a lot about him," I said. "Now may I please go and join the other kids?"

"Just so you are in by nine," Mom said firmly. "And please don't kid yourself that I didn't see what you did with your broccoli."

A Goat Hunt after dark feels a lot different from the way it feels when the sun is still shining. A dank chill seems to come up out of the ground and waver coldly around your ankles. Things that are alive, bugs and other creepy things, snap and tick and hum outside the circle of your flashlight. Noises rise and fall without reason, and a hollow sort of sound echoes after your footsteps.

When a pattering started in the trees above us, Zach looked up crossly. "Now don't tell me that it would go and rain on a Goat Hunt."

"All right, I won't," I replied, just as something cold and wet splatted on my nose. And then my left arm, and then the back of my neck.

By the time the rain started we were pretty far from our block. We had gone clear down to Ridge-

76

way at the end of the park. We started back, all hunched over with our sweaters pulled up over the backs of our necks. Not very many cars passed but the ones that did made a slick swish on the wet street, sometimes sending a spray of water up onto the sidewalk.

"Let's not go clear around the park," I suggested to Zach. "Let's cut through by the ball diamond. Maybe the goat found some good grass there, and anyway we won't be drowned every time a car goes by."

We know every inch of that park by daylight. Night and the weather had changed it into something different and strange. The steady drumming of the rain everywhere gave me a feeling of being surrounded. I never actually saw anything move inside the beam from that flashlight but I always felt that, just beyond that cone of yellow light, the shadows stirred frantically. I yelped like Edie when some bird in a tall tree startled awake to yell in a rough voice and swoop off through the trees with a great rhythmic flapping of wings.

And there were eyes. Yellow eyes peering at us, catching the beam of the light and then fading away as if they were just watchers, eyes that hung there in the darkness without even being attached to any animal. The bushes rustled and the low rumble of thunder sounded far off.

"I hate goats," Zach said in a sudden fierce voice when a twig snapped really loud near the walk. "I hate goats and I hate Goat Hunts and my jeans are wet clear to the knee."

I thought of kidding him about being a vet who hated animals. I even thought of kidding him about being afraid in a plain old neighborhood place like Ridgeway Park, but I didn't.

I was glad he was scared. I am that kind of kid that likes to do things with my friends. If I was going to race through that spooky wet park like a scared rabbit, I was just plain grateful to have old rabbit Zach scurrying along beside me.

Friday

At least Zach and I weren't the only quitters. When we finally got out of that park and over to Amy's house, we found a note fastened to her door.

GOAT HUNT CALLED ON ACCOUNT OF RAIN.
EVERYBODY GO HOME!

Zach groaned. "How is a person going to be able to sleep with tame animals roaming the night all around him?"

I don't know about him but for me it was easy. Mom made me put all my stuff in the dryer and turn it on high. My tennis shoes were still running and bumping the way they do when I went to sleep. I could hardly get myself to stop sleeping Friday morning in time for school.

The rest of the kids must have felt the same way because nobody talked much all the way there. Zach was seven minutes later than he usually is. Miss Button just sighed when he came in.

But Chester was there on time. He arrived wearing a red-and-black rugby sock on his right foot and that bright green one on his left. For once he wasn't smiling.

Miss Button handed back our papers about our interesting experiences. She must not have been as bored by my story about camping in Canada as I was. She had managed to stay awake long enough to make eight red circles where there should have been periods and underline the capital letters that I had left small.

Then she assigned a new story in our reading book. I groaned because I had been dreading that story ever since we got those books. The illustration was a picture of a green Martian stepping out of a spaceship that had landed in a murky dark cloud. It seems to me that if grown-ups want young scientists like me to get interested in the space program, they could do something about pictures like that. What kid in his right mind is going to want to hop around in a big balloon suit and live on dried food to meet some person who looks for all the world like broccoli set up on its feet to walk?

I opened my book to the first page and angled my head just right so that I could stare out the window and not be caught at it. From my chair I could see the very edge of the school yard out in front. I could see the bottom of the flagpole and those white lines where the crossing guards walk the little kids across. Just on the other side of the street is a white house with a big porch and a whole hedge of bushes that turn yellow in the spring.

I was just staring, not looking at anything at all, when something stirred in those bushes. I was squinting to see better when something shaped a little like a bunch of yellow grapes came out from between the leaves of the hedge. Actually, it was skinnier than a bunch of grapes and it looked hairy. I must have stared at it several seconds before I realized it was a beard that was fastened to a long yellow face.

I had in my mind that Chester's goat, Tui, was going to look like those little pygmy goats I had petted at the zoo. I had in my mind a sort of cuddly little thing with black spots on sleek white hair. I could even see the way my red bandanna had waggled back and forth as he ate it.

But this thing, this bearded yellow animal with the curled horns that was peering out through the bushes, was taller than a first grader. Its face looked a foot long and its jaw waggled back and forth like the clapper on a giant bell.

I forgot where I was.

"Tui," I shouted, still frozen in my seat. "Tui is out there."

That Chester wasn't frozen. He must have had his left foot with the green sock for *Go* already on the floor ready to run. He was across that room before the words were all the way out of my mouth. The rest of the kids started straining up in their seats and chattering and jabbering all at once.

"Jamie," Miss Button called out, in that I-don't-believe-what-is-going-on voice of hers. I kept trying to point and explain and watch Tui all at once. There was no way I could make her understand. My words were just falling all over themselves like the kids were doing racing for the window.

"Goat. . . . Tui. . . . Chester," I kept chattering.

Miss Button looked to Chester for help but he was already halfway toward the door. By the time she got her question out the door slammed behind him. I could hear the thump of his feet running down the hall right under that large sign that says:

RUNNING IN THE HALLS IS STRICTLY FORBIDDEN.

All us kids were up at Miss Button's desk in a minute. Edie and Amy and Zach and George and I had her all the way hemmed in.

"Please can we help?" we begged.

"He needs us,"

"Come on, please let us go."

She was shaking her head and motioning us to get back to our seats. And all that time I could hear the rest of the class at the window saying, "Oh, wow," or "Look at that!" and other stuff that would make even a teacher curious.

Then she gave up.

"All right," she shouted over our voices. "But hurry back from your . . ." She faltered. "Just hurry back."

By the time the rest of us got to the front door of the school, Chester was out at the edge of the street. Cars kept going past both ways so that Chester couldn't get across. You could see he was dancing up and down with impatience, that green sock just shining. Tui didn't look very excited at all. She was standing clear out in the yard now where everyone could see her. She looked as big as a pony with her great big ears lopping out at the sides and her horns, pale and curly, kind of shining in the sun.

She waggled her beard at Chester and cried, "*Baaaa*," in a really friendly tone. Then she ducked her head so that I could see the loop of frayed rope still hanging around her neck and started walking toward Chester. I could tell by the way she was staring at him that she wasn't paying any attention to the traffic that was passing in the street.

Just as she started to step down off the curb and

start toward Chester, we all heard the squeal of tires and a car started around the corner coming really fast.

It was a blue car.

It was Wally Parsons' blue sedan going about a hundred times faster than the twenty miles an hour that is posted in the school zone.

"Oh, no," Edie gasped behind me.

"Save the goat," Zach cried.

"It's Wally Parsons," George said in a tone of horror. "That street will be curb-to-curb goat."

Suddenly everything in the world seemed to slow down. We all held our breaths. It was as if we were watching one of those old silent horror movies on television. Tui was still walking toward Chester and the car was speeding toward the spot where Tui would walk.

Chester was shouting helplessly. "Halt, Tui!" he shouted. "Stop, Tui! Go back, Tui!" He was yelling at the top of his lungs. He might as well have been whispering for all the attention Tui paid to his commands.

All sorts of things went through my mind in about a minute.

Maybe Tui would pick up speed and get across the street before Wally got there.

Maybe Tui would hear his master's voice and stop in time.

And maybe, just maybe, that bully Wally Parsons would see Tui and put his foot on the brake as hard as he always puts it down on the gas pedal.

Then Tui saw the car. Everybody in that whole school yard breathed a sigh of relief as she stopped dead still and stared at the oncoming automobile. Her jaws quit waggling back and forth, and she had a little piece of that yellow hedge still sticking out between her teeth. Then she straightened her head up and gave her beard a little jerk. Dropping the leaves from her mouth, she said, *"Baaaa,"* in a strangely delighted tone.

"No," Chester screamed. "No, Tui. Don't do it. Don't do it!"

Eleanor had told us that Tui only ran when she chased cars. She hadn't really gone into how fast Tui ran when she was doing it. She might be Chester's goat but she sure didn't need any system to figure out which foot to put down first. She just lit out after Wally Parsons' car with one little hoof after another in a quick drumbeat. She aimed herself at that blue sedan like a rocket-powered missile.

As fast as Wally was driving, she still caught up with him in a quick clatter of goat hooves. She passed

the back wheels with her beard flying and ran right up to the window on the driver's side of the car. Her ears flopped and that beard just flew as she bleated at Wally Parsons with a loud, excited cry.

I guess when Wally saw that face looking into his window, that long yellow face with the horns and the beard and the wide-set yellow eyes, he really hit the gas to try to get away. He picked up speed and so did Tui. Wally Parsons hit the gas some more, and somehow it must have slipped his mind that it isn't enough to go fast, you have to steer, too.

That was the loudest crash I have ever heard in my life. Waves of sound wiggled up and down in my ears even after the crash was all over. There was the scrunch of metal, and a splitting sound when the telephone pole bent in the middle with big jagged splinters sticking out the side.

Then, after the big noise died, there was a sort of musical shower of sound as the glass of Wally's windshield slid off the hood and chimed against the hard surface of the road.

Tui stopped at the same moment that the car did. She stood still and stared at it with a very peaceful look. Then her jaws began to waggle back and forth like a kid with gum in her mouth. Chester was right there, hugging her long thick neck and talking softly to her. You could tell how much she liked him by the way she ducked her head and rubbed one ear against his face.

Miss Button can be pretty cross sometimes but she isn't stupid. She had given up and let all the rest of the class follow us kids out into the school yard. They all stood there in a cluster watching Wally Parsons tug at his damaged door before he finally got it to swing open. They watched as he got out of the car and stood up. He stood there for a long minute, looking at his blue sedan and the broken telephone pole. Then he seemed to swell up as he turned to Chester and Tui.

"I'll sue," he yelled. "I'll get you for this, you'll see."

"She didn't mean any harm," Chester said. His voice sounded a little worried and apologetic.

"Look at my car," Wally Parsons screamed. He started toward Chester and Tui with his fists balled up and his shoulders all hunched over. "I ought to beat your head in, you stupid jerk. You and that goat. You wait, you just wait, I'll sue . . ."

Wally had been too busy to look around and see that a police car had pulled in behind him. But the rest of us had seen it, and we waited.

The policeman got out very calmly. He stretched a little as he looked at the car and the telephone pole and Wally standing there screaming at Chester. Then he walked over and began writing something on a pad while he stared at the back of Wally Parsons' car.

"I'm going to call the cops on you, too," Wally was shouting at Chester. "You just wait and see."

"Is your name Wally Parsons?" the policeman asked, coming up behind him.

Wally whirled and stared. Then he nodded. He opened his mouth to yell at the policeman too but he didn't get a chance.

"We had a complaint called in on your speed in the school zone," the policeman said in this quiet voice. "I got here in time to check it back there. My radar gun registered you at thirty-seven miles an hour in a twenty-mile zone. Of course, that was before you speeded up to outrun the goat here."

"Then you saw it," Wally Parsons cried. "You saw that goat attack my car."

The policeman shook his head. "That's not what I saw. I saw you turn the corner into the school zone at excessive speed. I saw an animal chase your speeding car. I saw you lose control of the car and hit a telephone pole." He glanced up at the pole, which angled like a bicyclist's arm signaling a right turn. "I saw your car strike the pole with sufficient force to damage both the vehicle and the property of the telephone company."

"But that goat was chasing my car!" Wally yelled.

The policeman turned to Chester. "Is this your animal?"

"Yes, sir," Chester replied, nodding but not smiling. "I guess it is really the pet of all our family."

The policeman nodded. "We have a leash law for dogs. When a dog chases a car, it is considered a public nuisance. It just happens that we don't have any leash law for goats. But I recommend that this goat be penned off the public streets."

Chester was nodding and mumbling, "Yes, sir. We will, sir," but the policeman had already turned away.

"I would like to see your operator's license," he told Wally Parsons.

"But you can't . . . his goat. . . ." Wally was spluttering as he was also fishing in his back pocket for his wallet.

Miss Button tried to quiet the cheer that went up from the whole class but she didn't have any luck. We all tried to get her to let us wait and see the tow truck haul Wally Parsons' blue sedan away but she told us, "Enough is enough, you rascals."

She did excuse Chester to take Tui back home. Zach lent him his belt to use as a leash and Amy and Edie and I all picked grass and gave it to Tui while Chester was getting the belt adjusted just right. We were careful to stay in front of Tui while we picked grass because of what Eleanor had told us.

Before Chester had even taken Tui across the street, the bell rang for recess. Miss Button just sighed. "I give up," she said and waved us over onto the playground.

Mr. Allen was hopping around with his whistle swinging against his chest trying to get a game together. The kids wouldn't even look at him or his ball that kept bouncing under his left hand without his even looking at it. All they wanted to do was cluster around and talk about Chester and the goat.

"That Chester is going to be some kind of a hero in this town," somebody said. "My dad says that anyone who gets Wally Parsons off the street should get the keys to the city."

"He already was some kind of hero," George said right out. "Don't you remember how he won the foot race the first day he even came to school here? He's the fastest runner in Millard C. Fillmore School, maybe the world—who knows?"

"He lives up at the top of our hill," Amy chimed in. "Right in our neighborhood and there are eight kids in the family. Eight!"

"And the twin babies are so bald that they don't even have eyebrows," Edie added. "With polka dots, too."

I thought about mentioning his freckles and I'm

sure that Zach was ready to put in something about his animals but it was unnecessary. If they all hadn't seen Chester's freckles standing out with fear when his goat nearly crossed the street into the path of Wally Parsons' car, they hadn't seen anything that happened.

That Abbie who wears braces and has long legs like a stork and runs so fast was staring at us five kids enviously. "It must be really super to be friends with somebody like that Chester."

"It's not the end of the world," Zach said with a grin, hitching at his jeans which kept sliding down since he gave up his belt to be a goat rope.

Us kids just looked at each other and grinned the way Chester does all the time, while Mr. Allen went on yelling:

"All right, all right, all right . . ."

ABOUT THE AUTHOR

Mary Francis Shura has written over twenty books for young people. Born in Kansas, not far from Dodge City, the author has lived in many parts of the United States, including California and Massachusetts. Both of her parents came from early settler families of Missouri.

Aside from writing fiction for young readers and adults, Mary Francis Shura enjoys tennis, chess, reading, and cooking—especially making bread.

The author is married and the mother of a son, Dan, and three daughters, Minka, Ali, and Shay. She currently makes her home in the western suburbs of Chicago, in the village of Willowbrook.

ABOUT THE ARTIST

Susan Swan was born in Coral Gables and received the degree of M.F.A. with Honors from Florida State University. She has illustrated text and trade books, and lives in Westport, Connecticut.